My Buried Treasure

Richard Harding Davis

Contents

MY BURIED TREASURE

BY

Richard Harding Davis

MY BURIED TREASURE
by Richard Harding Davis

This is a true story of a search for buried treasure. The only part that is not true is the name of the man with whom I searched for the treasure. Unless I keep his name out of it he will not let me write the story, and, as it was his expedition and as my share of the treasure is only what I can make by writing the story, I must write as he dictates. I think the story should be told, because our experience was unique, and might be of benefit to others. And, besides, I need the money.

There is, however, no agreement preventing me from describing him as I think he is, or reporting, as accurately as I can, what he said and did as he said and did it.

For purposes of identification I shall call him Edgar Powell. The last name has no significance; but the first name is not chosen at random. The leader of our expedition, the head and brains of it, was and is the sort of man one would address as Edgar. No one would think of calling him "Ed," or "Eddie," any more than he would consider slapping him on the back.

We were together at college; but, as six hundred other boys were there at the same time, that gives no clew to his identity. Since those days, until he came to see me about the treasure, we had not met. All I knew of him was that he had succeeded his father in manufacturing unshrinkable flannels. Of course, the reader understands that is not the article of commerce he manufactures; but it is near enough, and it suggests the line of business to which he gives his life's blood. It is not similar to my own line of work, and in consequence, when he wrote me, on the unshrinkable flannels official writing-paper, that he wished to see me in reference to a matter of business of "mutual benefit," I was considerably puzzled.

A few days later, at nine in the morning, an hour of his own choosing, he came to my rooms in New York City.

Except that he had grown a beard, he was as I remembered him, thin and tall, but with no chest, and stooping shoulders. He wore eye-glasses, and as of old through these he regarded you disapprovingly and warily as though he suspected you might try to borrow money, or even joke with him. As with Edgar I had never felt any temptation to do either, this was irritating.

But from force of former habit we greeted each other by our first names, and he suspiciously accepted a cigar. Then, after fixing me both with his eyes and with his eye-glasses and swearing me to secrecy, he began abruptly.

"Our mills," he said, "are in New Bedford; and I own several small cottages there and in Fairhaven. I rent them out at a moderate rate. The other day one of my tenants, a Portuguese sailor, was taken suddenly ill and sent for me. He had made many voyages in and out of Bedford to the South Seas, whaling, and he told me on his last voyage he had touched at his former home at Teneriffe. There his grandfather had given him a document that had been left him by his father. His grandfather said it contained an important secret, but one that was of value only in America, and that when he returned to that continent he must be very careful to whom he showed it. He told me it was written in a kind of English he could not understand, and that he had been afraid to let any one see it. He wanted me to accept the document in payment of the rent he owed me, with the understanding that I was not to look at it, and that if he got well I was to give it back. If he pulled through, he was to pay me in some other way; but if he died I was to keep the document. About a month ago he died, and I examined the paper. It purports to tell where there is buried a pirate's treasure. And," added Edgar, gazing at me severely and as though he challenged me to contradict him, "I intend to dig for it!"

Had he told me he contemplated crossing the Rocky Mountains in a Baby Wright, or leading a cotillon, I could not have been more astonished. I am afraid I laughed aloud.

"You!" I exclaimed. "Search for buried treasure?"

My tone visibly annoyed him. Even the eye-glasses radiated disapproval.

"I see nothing amusing in the idea," Edgar protested coldly. "It is a plain business proposition. I find the outlay will be small, and if I am successful the returns should be large; at a rough estimate about one million dollars."

Even to-day, no true American, at the thought of one million dollars, can remain covered. His letter to me had said, "for our mutual benefit." I became respectful and polite, I might even say abject. After all, the ties that bind us in those dear old college days are not lightly to be disregarded.

"If I can be of any service to you, Edgar, old man," I assured him heartily, "if I can help you find it, you know I shall be only too happy." With regret I observed that my generous offer did not seem to deeply move him.

"I came to you in this matter," he continued stiffly, "because you seemed to be the sort of person who would be interested in a search for buried treasure."

"I am," I exclaimed. "Always have been."

"Have you," he demanded searchingly, "any practical experience?"

I tried to appear at ease; but I knew then just how the man who applies to look after your furnace feels, when you ask him if he can also run a sixty horse-power dynamo.

"I have never actually FOUND any buried treasure," I admitted; "but I know where lots of it is, and I know just how to go after it." I endeavored to dazzle him with expert knowledge.

"Of course," I went on airily, "I am familiar with all the expeditions that have tried for the one on Cocos Island, and I know all about the Peruvian treasure on Trinidad, and the lost treasures of Jalisco near Guadalajara, and the sunken galleon on the Grand Cayman, and when I was on the Isle of Pines I had several very tempting offers to search there. And the late Captain Boynton invited me----"

"But," interrupted Edgar in a tone that would tolerate no trifling, "you yourself have never financed or organized an expedition with the object in view of----"

"Oh, that part's easy!" I assured him. "The fitting-out part you can safely leave to me." I assumed a confidence that I hoped he might believe was real. "There's always a tramp steamer in the Erie Basin," I said, "that one can charter for any kind of adventure, and I have the addresses of enough soldiers of fortune, filibusters, and professional revolutionists to man a battle-ship, all fine fellows in a tight corner. And I'll promise you they'll follow us to hell, and back----"

"That!" exclaimed Edgar, "is exactly what I feared!"

"I beg your pardon!" I exclaimed.

"That's exactly what I DON'T want," said Edgar sternly. "I don't INTEND to get into any tight corners. I don't WANT to go to hell!"

I saw that in my enthusiasm I had perhaps alarmed him. I continued more temperately.

"Any expedition after treasure," I pointed out, "is never without risk. You must have discipline, and you must have picked men. Suppose there's a mutiny? Suppose they try to rob us of the treasure on our way home? We must have men we can rely on, and men who know how to pump a Winchester. I can get you both. And Bannerman will furnish me with anything from a pair of leggins to a quick firing gun, and on Clark Street they'll quote me a special rate on ship stores, hydraulic pumps, divers' helmets----"

Edgar's eye-glasses became frosted with cold, condemnatory scorn. He shook his head disgustedly.

"I was afraid of this!" he murmured.

I endeavored to reassure him.

"A little danger," I laughed, "only adds to the fun."

"I want you to understand," exclaimed Edgar indignantly, "there isn't going to be any danger. There isn't going to be any fun. This is a plain business proposition. I asked you those questions just to test you. And you approached the matter exactly as I feared you would. I was prepared for it. In fact," he explained shamefacedly, "I've read several of your little stories, and I find they run to adventure and blood and thunder; they are not of the analytical school of fiction. Judging from them," he added accusingly, "you have a tendency to the romantic." He spoke reluctantly as though saying I had a tendency to epileptic fits or the morphine habit.

"I am afraid," I was forced to admit, "that to me pirates and buried treasure always suggest adventure. And your criticism of my writings is well observed. Others have discovered the same fatal weakness. We cannot all," I pointed out, "manufacture unshrinkable flannels."

At this compliment to his more fortunate condition, Edgar seemed to soften.

"I grant you," he said, "that the subject has almost invariably been approached from the point of view you take. And what," he demanded triumphantly, "has been the result? Failure, or at least, before success was attained, a most unnecessary and regrettable loss of blood and life. Now, on my expedition, I do not intend that any blood shall be shed, or that anybody shall lose his life. I have not entered into this matter hastily. I have taken out information, and mean to benefit by other people's mistakes. When I decided to go on with this," he explained, "I read all the books that bear on searches for buried treasure, and I found that in each case the same mistakes were made, and that then, in order to remedy the mistakes, it was invariably necessary to kill somebody. Now, by not making those mistakes, it will not be necessary for me to kill any one, and nobody is going to have a chance to kill me.

"You propose that we fit out a schooner and sign on a crew. What will happen? A man with a sabre cut across his forehead, or with a black patch over one eye, will inevitably be one of that crew. And, as soon as we sail, he will at once begin to plot against us. A cabin boy who the conspirators think is asleep in his bunk will overhear their plot and will run to the quarter-deck to give warning; but a pistol shot rings out, and the cabin boy falls at the foot of the companion ladder. The cabin boy is always the first one to go. After that the mutineers kill the first mate, and lock us in our cabin, and take over the ship. They will then broach a cask of rum, and all through the night we will listen to their drunken howlings, and from the cabin airport watch the body of the first mate rolling in the lee scuppers."

"But you forget," I protested eagerly, "there is always ONE faithful member of the crew, who----"

Edgar interrupted me impatiently.

"I have not overlooked him," he said. "He is a Jamaica negro of gigantic proportions, or the ship's cook; but he always gets his too, and he gets it good. They throw HIM to the sharks! Then we all camp out on a desert island inhabited only by goats, and we build a stockade, and the mutineers come to treat with us under a white flag, and we, trusting entirely to their honor, are fools enough to go out and talk with them. At which they shoot us up, and withdraw laughing scornfully." Edgar fixed his eye-glasses upon me accusingly.

"Am I right, or am I wrong?" he demanded. I was unable to answer. "The only man," continued Edgar warmly, "who ever showed the slightest intelligence in the matter was the fellow in the 'Gold Bug'. HE kept his mouth shut. He never let any one know that he was after buried treasure, until he found it. That's me! Now I know EXACTLY where this treasure is, and----"

I suppose, involuntarily, I must have given a start of interest; for Edgar paused and shook his head, slyly and cunningly. "And if you think I have the map on my person now," he declared in triumph, "you'll have to guess again!"

"Really," I protested, "I had no intention----"

"Not you, perhaps," said Edgar grudgingly; "but your Japanese valet conceals himself behind those curtains, follows me home, and at night----"

"I haven't got a valet," I objected.

Edgar merely smiled with the most aggravating self-sufficiency. "It makes no difference," he declared. "NO ONE will ever find that map, or see that map, or know where that treasure is, until I point to the spot."

"Your caution is admirable," I said; "but what," I jeered, "makes you think you can point to the spot, because your map says something like, 'Through the Sunken Valley to Witch's Caldron, four points N. by N. E. to Gallows Hill where the shadow falls at sunrise, fifty fathoms west, fifty paces north as the crow flies, to the Seven Wells'? How the deuce," I demanded, "is any one going to point to that spot?"

"It isn't that kind of map," shouted Edgar triumphantly. "If it had been, I wouldn't have gone on with it. It's a map anybody can read except a half-caste Portuguese sailor. It's as plain as a laundry bill. It says," he paused apprehensively, and then continued with caution, "it says at such and such a place there is a something. So many somethings from that something are three what-you-may-call-'ems, and in the centre of these three what-you-may-call-'ems is buried the treasure. It's as plain as that!"

"Even with the few details you have let escape you," I said, "I could find THAT spot in my sleep."

"I don't think you could," said Edgar uncomfortably; but I could see that he had mentally warned himself to be less communicative. "And," he went on, "I am willing to lead you to it, if you subscribe to certain conditions."

Edgar's insulting caution had ruffled my spirit.

"Why do you think you can trust ME?" I asked haughtily. And then, remembering my share of the million dollars, I added in haste, "I accept the conditions."

"Of course, as you say, one has got to take SOME risk," Edgar continued; "but I feel sure," he said, regarding me doubtfully, "you would not stoop to open robbery." I thanked him.

"Well, until one is tempted," said Edgar, "one never knows WHAT he might do. And I've simply GOT to have one other man, and I picked on you because I thought you could write about it."

"I see," I said, "I am to act as the historian of the expedition."

"That will be arranged later," said Edgar. "What I chiefly want you for is to dig. Can you dig?" he asked eagerly. I told him I could; but that I would rather do almost anything else.

"I MUST have one other man," repeated Edgar, "a man who is strong enough to dig, and strong enough to resist the temptation to murder me." The retort was so easy that I let it pass. Besides, on Edgar, it would have been wasted.

"I THINK you will do," he said with reluctance. "And now the conditions!"

I smiled agreeably.

"You are already sworn to secrecy," said Edgar. "And you now agree in every detail to obey me implicitly, and to accompany me to a certain place, where you will dig. If I find the treasure, you agree, to help me guard it, and convey it to wherever I decide it is safe to leave it. Your responsibility is then at an end. One year after the treasure is discovered, you will be free to write the account of the expedition. For what you write, some magazine may pay you. What it pays you will be your share of the treasure."

Of my part of the million dollars, which I had hastily calculated could not be less than one-fifth, I had already spent over one hundred thousand dollars and was living far beyond my means. I had bought a farm with a waterfront on the Sound, a motor-boat, and, as I was not sure which make I preferred, three automobiles. I had at my own, expense produced a play of mine that no manager had appreciated, and its name in electric lights was already blinding Broadway. I had purchased a Hollander express rifle, a REAL amber cigar holder, a private secretary who could play both rag-time and tennis, and a fur coat. So Edgar's generous offer left me naked. When I had again accustomed myself to the narrow confines of my flat, and the jolt of the surface cars, I asked humbly:

"Is that ALL I get?"

"Why should you expect any more?" demanded Edgar. "It isn't YOUR treasure. You wouldn't expect me to make you a present of an interest in my mills; why should you get a share of my treasure?" He gazed at me reproachfully. "I thought you'd be pleased," he said. "It must be hard to think of things to write about, and I'm giving you a subject for nothing. I thought," he remonstrated, "you'd jump at the chance. It isn't every day a man can dig for buried treasure."

"That's all right," I said. "Perhaps I appreciate that quite as well as you do. But my time has a certain small value, and I can't leave my work just for excitement. We may be weeks, months---- How long do you think we----"

Behind his eye-glasses Edgar winked reprovingly.

"That is a leading question," he said. "I will pay all your legitimate expenses--transportation, food, lodging. It won't cost you a cent. And you write the story--with my name left out," he added hastily; "it would hurt my standing in the trade," he explained--"and get paid for it."

I saw a sea voyage at Edgar's expense. I saw palm leaves, coral reefs. I felt my muscles aching and the sweat run from my neck and shoulders as I drove my pick into the chest of gold.

"I'll go with you!" I said. We shook hands on it. "When do we start?" I asked.

"Now!" said Edgar. I thought he wished to test me; he had touched upon one of my pet vanities.

"You can't do that with me!" I said. "My bags are packed and ready for any place in the wide world, except the cold places. I can start this minute. Where is it, the Gold Coast, the Ivory Coast, the Spanish Main----"

Edgar frowned inscrutably. "Have you an empty suit-case?" he asked.

"Why EMPTY?" I demanded.

"To carry the treasure," said Edgar. "I left mine in the hall. We will need two."

"And your trunks?" I said.

"There aren't going to be any trunks," said Edgar. From his pocket he had taken a folder of the New Jersey Central Railroad. "If we hurry," he exclaimed, "we can catch the ten-thirty express, and return to New York in time for dinner."

"And what about the treasure?" I roared.

"We'll' bring it with us," said Edgar.

I asked for information. I demanded confidences. Edgar refused both. I insisted that I might be allowed at least to carry my automatic pistol. "Suppose some one tries to take the treasure from us?" I pointed out.

"No one," said Edgar severely, "would be such an ass as to imagine we are carrying buried treasure in a suit-case. He will think it contains pajamas."

"For local color, then," I begged, "I want to say in my story that I went heavily armed."

"Say it, then," snapped Edgar. "But you can't DO it! Not with me, you can't! How do I know you mightn't----" He shook his head warily.

It was a day in early October, the haze of Indian summer was in the air, and as we crossed the North River by the Twenty-third Street Ferry the sun flashed upon the white clouds overhead and the tumbling waters below. On each side of us great vessels with the Blue Peter at the fore lay at the wharfs ready to cast off, or were already nosing their way down the channel toward strange and beautiful ports. Lamport and Holt were rolling down to Rio; the Royal Mail's MAGDALENA, no longer "white and gold," was off to Kingston, where once seven pirates swung in chains; the CLYDE was on her way to Hayti where the buccaneers came from; the MORRO CASTLE was bound for Havana, which Morgan, king of all the pirates, had once made his own; and the RED D was steaming to Porto Cabello where Sir Francis Drake, as big a buccaneer as any of them, lies entombed in her harbor. And I was setting forth on a buried-treasure expedition on a snub-nosed, flat-bellied, fresh-water ferry-boat, bound for Jersey City! No one will ever know my sense of humiliation. And, when the Italian boy insulted my immaculate tan shoes by pointing at them and saying, "Shine?" I could have slain him. Fancy digging for buried treasure in freshly varnished boots! But Edgar did not mind. To him there was nothing lacking; it was just as it should be. He was deeply engrossed in calculating how many offices were for rent in the Singer Building!

When we reached the other side, he refused to answer any of my eager questions. He would not let me know even for what place on the line he had purchased our tickets, and, as a hint that I should not disturb him, he stuffed into my hands the latest magazines. "At least tell me this," I demanded. "Have you ever been to this place before to-day?"

"Once," said Edgar shortly, "last week. That's when I found out I would need some one with me who could dig."

"How do you know it's the RIGHT place?" I whispered.

The summer season was over, and of the chair car we were the only occupants; but, before he answered, Edgar looked cautiously round him and out of the window. We had just passed Red Bank.

"Because the map told me," he answered. "Suppose," he continued fretfully, "you had a map of New York City with the streets marked on it plainly? Suppose the map said that if you walked to where Broadway and Fifth Avenue meet, you would find the Flatiron Building. Do you think you could find it?"

"Was it as easy as THAT?" I gasped.

"It was as easy as THAT!" said Edgar.

I sank back into my chair and let the magazines slide to the floor. What fiction story was there in any one of them so enthralling as the actual possibilities that lay before me? In two hours I might be bending over a pot of gold, a sea chest stuffed with pearls and rubies!

I began to recall all the stories I had heard as a boy of treasure buried along the coast by Kidd on his return voyage from the Indies. Where along the Jersey sea-line were there safe harbors? The train on which we were racing south had its rail head at Barnegat Bay. And between Barnegat and Red Bank there now was but one other inlet, that of the Manasquan River. It might be Barnegat; it might be Manasquan. It could not be a great distance from either; toward the ocean down a broad, sandy road. The season had passed and the windows of the cottages and bungalows on either side of the road were barricaded with planks. On the verandas hammocks abandoned to the winds hung in tatters, on the back porches the doors of empty re-frigerators swung open on one hinge, and on every side above the fields of gorgeous golden-rod rose signs reading "For Rent." When we had progressed in silence for a mile, the sandy avenue lost itself in the deeper sand of the beach, and the horse of his own will came to a halt.

On one side we were surrounded by locked and deserted bathing houses, on the other by empty pavilions shuttered and barred against the winter, but still in-viting one to "Try our salt water taffy" or to "Keep cool with an ice-cream soda." Rupert turned and looked inquiringly at Edgar. To the north the beach stretched in an unbroken line to Manasquan Inlet. To the south three miles away we could see floating on the horizon-like a mirage the hotels and summer cottages of Bay Head.

"Drive toward the inlet," directed Edgar. "This gentleman and I will walk."

Relieved of our weight, the horse stumbled bravely into the trackless sand, while below on the damper and firmer shingle we walked by the edge of the wa-ter.

The tide was coming in and the spent waves, spreading before them an advance guard of tiny shells and pebbles, threatened our boots' and at the same time in soothing, lazy whispers warned us of their attack. These lisping murmurs and the crash and roar of each incoming wave as it broke were the only sounds. And on the beach we were the only human figures. At last the scene began to bear some resemblance to one set for an adventure. The rolling ocean, a coast steamer dragging a great column of black smoke, and cast high upon the beach the wreck of a schooner, her masts tilting drunkenly, gave color to our purpose. It became filled with greater promise of drama, more picturesque. I began to thrill with excitement. I regarded Edgar appealingly, in eager supplication. At last he broke the silence that was torturing me.

"We will now walk higher up," he commanded. "If we get our feet wet, we may take cold."

My spirit was too far broken to make reply. But to my relief I saw that in leaving the beach Edgar had some second purpose. With each heavy step he was drawing toward two high banks of sand in a hollow behind which, protected by the banks, were three stunted, wind-driven pines. His words came back to me.

"So many what-you-may-call-'ems." Were these pines the three somethings from something, the what-you-may-call-'ems? The thought chilled me to the spine. I gazed at them fascinated. I felt like falling on my knees in the sand and tearing their secret from them with my bare hands. I was strong enough to dig them up by the roots, strong enough to dig the Panama Canal! I glanced tremulously at Edgar. His eyes were wide open and, eloquent with dismay, his lower jaw had fallen. He turned and looked at me for the first time with consideration. Apology and remorse were written in every line of his countenance.

I'm sorry, he stammered. I had a cruel premonition. I exclaimed with distress.

"You have lost the map!" I hissed.

"No, no," protested Edgar; "but I entirely forgot to bring any lunch!"

With violent mutterings I tore off my upper and outer garments and tossed them into the hack.

"Where do I begin?" I asked.

Edgar pointed to a spot inside the triangle formed by the three trees and equally distant from each.

"Put that horse behind the bank," I commanded, "where no one can see him! And both you and Rupert keep off the sky-line!" From the north and south we were now all three hidden by the two high banks of sand; to the east lay the beach and the Atlantic Ocean, and to the west stretches of marshes that a mile away met a wood of pine trees and the railroad round-house.

I began to dig. I knew that weary hours lay before me, and I attacked the sand leisurely and with deliberation. It was at first no great effort; but as the hole grew in depth, and the roots of the trees were exposed, the work was sufficient for several men. Still, as Edgar had said, it is not every day that one can dig for treasure, and in thinking of what was to come I forgot my hands that quickly blistered, and my breaking back. After an hour I insisted that Edgar should take a turn; but he made such poor headway that my patience could not contain me, and I told him I was sufficiently rested and would continue. With alacrity he scrambled out of the hole, and, taking a cigar from my case, seated himself comfortably in the hack. I took my comfort in anticipating the thrill that would be mine when the spade would ring on the ironbound chest; when, with a blow of the axe, I would expose to view the hidden jewels, the pieces of eight, coated with verdigris, the string of pearls, the chains of yellow gold. Edgar had said a million dollars. That must mean there would be diamonds, many diamonds. I would hold them in my hands, watch them, at the sudden sunshine, blink their eyes and burst into tiny, burning fires. In imagination I would replace them in the setting, from which, years before, they had been stolen. I would try to guess whence they came from a jewelled chalice in some dim cathedral, from the breast of a great lady, from the hilt of an admiral's sword.

After another hour I lifted my aching shoulders and, wiping the sweat from my eyes, looked over the edge of the hole. Rupert, with his back to the sand-hill, was asleep. Edgar with one hand was waving away the mosquitoes and in the other was holding one of the magazines he had bought on the way down. I could even see the page upon which his eyes were riveted. It was an advertisement for breakfast food. In my indignation the spade slipped through my cramped and perspiring fingers, and as it struck the bottom of the pit, something--a band of iron, a steel lock, an iron ring--gave forth a muffled sound. My heart stopped beating as suddenly as though Mr. Corbett had hit it with his closed fist. My blood turned to melted ice. I drove the spade down as fiercely as though it was a dagger. It sank into rotten wood. I had made no sound; for I could hardly breathe. But the slight noise of the blow had reached Edgar. I heard the springs of the hack creak as he vaulted from it, and the next moment he was towering above me, peering down into the pit. His eyes were wide with excitement, greed, and fear. In his hands he clutched the two suit-cases. Like a lion defending his cubs he glared at me.

"Get out!" he shouted.

"Like hell!" I said.

"Get out!" he roared. "I'll do the rest. That's mine, not yours! GET OUT!"

With a swift kick I brushed away the sand. I found I was standing on a squat wooden box, bound with bands of rusty iron. I had only to stoop to touch it. It was so rotten that I could have torn it apart with my bare hands. Edgar was dancing on the edge of the pit, incidentally kicking sand into my mouth and nostrils.

"You PROMISED me!" he roared. "You PROMISED to obey me!"

"You ass!" I shouted. "Haven't I done all the work? Don't I get----"

"You get out!" roared Edgar.

Slowly, disgustedly, with what dignity one can display in crawling out of a sand-pit, I scrambled to the top.

"Go over there," commanded Edgar pointing, "and sit down."

In furious silence I seated myself beside Rupert. He was still slumbering and snoring happily. From where I sat I could see nothing of what was going forward in the pit, save once, when the head of Edgar, his eyes aflame and his hair and eye-glasses sprinkled with sand, appeared above it. Apparently he was fearful lest I had moved from the spot where he had placed me. I had not; but had he known my inmost feelings he would have taken the axe into the pit with him.

I must have sat so for half an hour. In the sky above me a fish-hawk drifted lazily. From the beach sounded the steady beat of the waves, and from the town across the marshes came the puffing of a locomotive and the clanging bells of the freight trains. The breeze from the sea cooled the sweat on my aching body; but it could not cool the rage in my heart. If I had the courage of my feelings, I would have cracked Edgar over head with the spade, buried him in the pit, bribed Rupert, and forever after lived happily on my ill-gotten gains. That was how Kidd, or Morgan, or Blackbeard would have acted. I cursed the effete civilization which had taught me to want many pleasures but had left me with a conscience that would not let me take human life to obtain them, not even Edgar's life.

In half an hour a suit-case was lifted into view and dropped on the edge of the pit. It was followed by the other, and then by Edgar. Without asking me to help him, because he probably knew I would not, he shovelled the sand into the hole, and then placed the suitcases in the carriage. With increasing anger I observed that the contents of each were so heavy that to lift it he used both hands.

"There is no use your asking any questions," he announced, "because I won't answer them."

I gave him minute directions as to where he could go; but instead we drove in black silence to the station. There Edgar rewarded Rupert with a dime, and while we waited for the train to New York placed the two suit-cases against the wall of the ticket office and sat upon them. When the train arrived he warned me in a hoarse whisper that I had promised to help him guard the treasure, and gave me one of the suit-cases. It weighed a ton. Just to spite Edgar, I had a plan to kick it open, so that every one on the platform might scramble for the contents. But again my infernal New England conscience restrained me.

Edgar had secured the drawing-room in the parlor-car, and when we were safely inside and the door bolted my curiosity became stronger than my pride.

"Edgar," I said, "your ingratitude is contemptible. Your suspicions are ridiculous; but, under these most unusual conditions, I don't blame you. But we are quite safe now. The door is fastened," I pointed out ingratiatingly, "it and this train doesn't stop for another forty minutes. I think this would be an excellent time to look at the treasure."

"I don't!" said Edgar.

I sank back into my chair. With intense enjoyment I imagined the train in which we were seated hurling itself into another train; and everybody, including Edgar, or, rather, especially Edgar, being instantly but painlessly killed. By such an act of an all-wise Providence I would at once become heir to one million dollars. It was a beautiful, satisfying dream. Even MY conscience accepted it with a smug smile. It was so vivid a dream that I sat guiltily expectant, waiting for the crash to come, for the shrieks and screams, for the rush of escaping steam and breaking window-panes.

But it was far too good to be true. Without a jar the train carried us and its precious burden in safety to the Jersey City terminal. And each, with half a million dollars in his hand, hurried to the ferry, assailed by porters, news-boys, hackmen. To them we were a couple of commuters saving a dime by carrying our own hand-bags.

It was now six o'clock, and I pointed out to Edgar that at that hour the only vaults open were those of the Night and Day Bank. And to that institution in a taxicab we at once made our way. I paid the chauffeur, and two minutes later, with a gasp of relief and rejoicing, I dropped the suit-case I had carried on a table in the steel-walled fastnesses of the vaults. Gathered excitedly around us were the officials of the bank, summoned hastily from above, and watchmen in plain clothes, and watchmen in uniforms of gray. Great bars as thick as my leg protected us. Walls of chilled steel rising from solid rock stood between our treasure and the outer world. Until then I had not known how tremendous the nervous strain had been; but now it came home to me. I mopped the perspiration from my forehead, I drew a deep breath.

"Edgar," I exclaimed happily, "I congratulate you!" I found Edgar extending toward me a two-dollar bill. "You gave the chauffeur two dollars,"' he said. "The fare was really one dollar eighty; so you owe me twenty cents."

Mechanically I laid two dimes upon the table.

"All the other expenses," continued Edgar, "which I agreed to pay, I have paid." He made a peremptory gesture. "I won't detain you any longer," he said. "Good-night!"

"Good-night!" I cried. "Don't I see the treasure?" Against the walls of chilled steel my voice rose like that of a tortured soul. "Don't I touch it!" I yelled. "Don't I even get a squint?"

Even the watchmen looked sorry for me.

"You do not!" said Edgar calmly. "You have fulfilled your part of the agreement. I have fulfilled mine. A year from now you can write the story." As I moved in a dazed state toward the steel door, his voice halted me.

"And you can say in your story," called Edgar, "that there is only one way to get a buried treasure. That is to go, and get it!"

THE CONSUL

For over forty years, in one part of the world or another, old man Marshall had, served his country as a United States consul. He had been appointed by Lincoln. For a quarter of a century that fact was his distinction. It was now his epitaph. But in former years, as each new administration succeeded the old, it had again and again saved his official head. When victorious and voracious place-hunters, searching the map of the world for spoils, dug out his hiding-place and demanded his consular sign as a reward for a younger and more aggressive party worker, the ghost of the dead President protected him. In the State Department, Marshall had become a tradition. "You can't touch Him!" the State Department would say; "why, HE was appointed by Lincoln!" Secretly, for this weapon against the hungry headhunters, the department was infinitely grateful. Old man Marshall was a consul after its own heart. Like a soldier, he was obedient, disciplined; wherever he was sent, there, without question, he would go. Never against exile, against ill-health, against climate did he make complaint. Nor when he was moved on and down to make way for some ne'er-do-well with influence, with a brother-in-law in the Senate, with a cousin owning a newspaper, with rich relatives who desired him to drink himself to death at the expense of the government rather than at their own, did old man Marshall point to his record as a claim for more just treatment.

And it had been an excellent record. His official reports, in a quaint, stately hand, were models of English; full of information, intelligent, valuable, well observed. And those few of his countrymen, who stumbled upon him in the out-of-the-world places to which of late he had been banished, wrote of him to the department in terms of admiration and awe. Never had he or his friends petitioned for promotion, until it was at last apparent that, save for his record and the memory of his dead patron, he had no friends. But, still in the department the tradition held and, though he was not advanced, he was not dismissed.

"If that old man's been feeding from the public trough ever since the Civil War," protested a "practical" politician, "it seems to me, Mr. Secretary, that he's about had his share. Ain't it time he give some one else a bite? Some of us that has, done the work, that has borne the brunt----"

"This place he now holds," interrupted the Secretary of State suavely, "is one hardly commensurate with services like yours. I can't pronounce the name of it, and I'm not sure just where it is, but I see that, of the last six consuls we sent there, three resigned within a month and the other three died of yellow-fever. Still, if you insist----"

The practical politician reconsidered hastily. "I'm not the sort," he protested, "to turn out a man appointed by our martyred President. Besides, he's so old now, if the fever don't catch him, he'll die of old age, anyway."

The Secretary coughed uncomfortably. "And they say," he murmured, "republics are ungrateful."

"I don't quite get that," said the practical politician.

Of Porto Banos, of the Republic of Colombia, where as consul Mr. Marshall was upholding the dignity of the United States, little could be said except that it possessed a sure harbor. When driven from the Caribbean Sea by stress of weather, the largest of ocean tramps, and even battle-ships, could find in its protecting arms of coral a safe shelter. But, as young Mr. Aiken, the wireless operator, pointed out, unless driven by a hurricane and the fear of death, no one ever visited it. Back of the ancient wharfs, that dated from the days when Porto Banos was a receiver of stolen goods for buccaneers and pirates, were rows of thatched huts, streets, according to the season, of dust or mud, a few iron-barred, jail-like barracks, customhouses, municipal buildings, and the whitewashed adobe houses of the consuls. The backyard of the town was a swamp. Through this at five each morning a rusty engine pulled a train of flat cars to the base of the mountains, and, if meanwhile the rails had not disappeared into the swamp, at five in the evening brought back the flat cars laden with odorous coffee-sacks.

In the daily life of Porto Banos, waiting for the return of the train, and betting if it would return, was the chief interest. Each night the consuls, the foreign residents, the wireless operator, the manager of the rusty railroad met for dinner. There at the head of the long table, by virtue of his years, of his courtesy and distinguished manner, of his office, Mr. Marshall presided. Of the little band of exiles he was the chosen ruler. His rule was gentle. By force of example he had made existence in Porto Banos more possible. For women and children Porto Banos was a death-trap, and before "old man Marshall" came there had been no influence to remind the enforced bachelors of other days.

They had lost interest, had grown lax, irritable, morose. Their white duck was seldom white. Their cheeks were unshaven. When the sun sank into the swamp and the heat still turned Porto Banos into a Turkish bath, they threw dice on the greasy tables of the Cafe Bolivar for drinks. The petty gambling led to petty quarrels; the drinks to fever. The coming of Mr. Marshall changed that. His standard of life, his tact, his worldly wisdom, his cheerful courtesy, his fastidious personal neatness shamed the younger men; the desire to please him, to, stand well in his good opinion, brought back pride and self-esteem.

The lieutenant of her Majesty's gun-boat PLOVER noted the change.

"Used to be," he exclaimed, "you couldn't get out of the Cafe Bolivar without some one sticking a knife in you; now it's a debating club. They all sit round a table and listen to an old gentleman talk world politics."

If Henry Marshall brought content to the exiles of Porto Banos, there was little in return that Porto Banos could give to him. Magazines and correspondents in six languages kept him in touch with those foreign lands in which he had represented his country, but of the country he had represented, newspapers and periodicals showed him only too clearly that in forty years it had grown away from him, had changed beyond recognition.

When last he had called at the State Department, he had been made to feel he was a man without a country, and when he visited his home town in Vermont, he was looked upon as a Rip Van Winkle. Those of his boyhood friends who were not dead had long thought of him as dead. And the sleepy, pretty village had become a bustling commercial centre. In the lanes where, as a young man, he had walked among wheatfields, trolley-cars whirled between rows of mills and factories. The children had grown to manhood, with children of their own.

Like a ghost, he searched for house after house, where once he had been made welcome, only to find in its place a towering office building. "All had gone, the old familiar faces." In vain he scanned even the shop fronts for a friendly, homelike name. Whether the fault was his, whether he would better have served his own interests than those of his government, it now was too late to determine. In his own home, he was a stranger among strangers. In the service he had so faithfully followed, rank by rank, he had been dropped, until now he, who twice had been a consul-general, was an exile, banished to a fever swamp. The great Ship of State had dropped him overside, had "marooned" him, and sailed away.

Twice a day he walked along the shell road to the Cafe Bolivar, and back again to the consulate. There, as he entered the outer office, Jose, the Colombian clerk, would rise and bow profoundly.

"Any papers for me to sign, Jose?" the consul would ask.

"Not to-day, Excellency," the clerk would reply. Then Jose would return to writing a letter to his lady-love; not that there was any-thing to tell her, but because writing on the official paper of the consulate gave him importance in his eyes, and in hers. And in the inner office the consul would continue to gaze at the empty harbor, the empty coral reefs, the empty, burning sky.

The little band of exiles were at second break fast when the wireless man came in late to announce that a Red D. boat and the island of Curacao had both reported a hurricane coming north. Also, that much concern was felt for the safety of the yacht SERAPIS. Three days before, in advance of her coming, she had sent a wireless to Wilhelmstad, asking the captain of the port to reserve a berth for her. She expected to arrive the following morning. But for forty-eight hours nothing had been heard from her, and it was believed she had been overhauled by the hurricane. Owing to the presence on board of Senator Hanley, the closest friend of the new President, the man who had made him president, much concern was felt at Washington. To try to pick her up by wireless, the gun-boat NEWARK had been ordered from Culebra, the cruiser RALEIGH, with Admiral Hardy on board, from Colon. It was possible she would seek shelter at Porto Banos. The consul was ordered to report.

As Marshall wrote out his answer, the French consul exclaimed with interest:

"He is of importance, then, this senator?" he asked. "Is it that in your country ships of war are at the service of a senator?"

Aiken, the wireless operator, grinned derisively.

"At the service of THIS senator, they are!" he answered. "They call him the 'king-maker,' the man behind the throne."

"But in your country," protested the Frenchman, "there is no throne. I thought your president was elected by the people?"

"That's what the people think," answered Aiken. "In God's country," he explained, "the trusts want a rich man in the Senate, with the same interests as their own, to represent them. They chose Hanley. He picked out of the candidates for the presidency the man he thought would help the interests. He nominated him, and the people voted for him. Hanley is what we call a 'boss.'"

The Frenchman looked inquiringly at Marshall.

"The position of the boss is the more dangerous," said Marshall gravely, "because it is unofficial, because there are no laws to curtail his powers. Men like Senator Hanley are a menace to good government. They see in public office only a reward for party workers."

"That's right," assented Aiken. "Your forty years' service, Mr. Consul, wouldn't count with Hanley. If he wanted your job, he'd throw you out as quick as he would a drunken cook."

Mr. Marshall flushed painfully, and the French consul hastened to interrupt.

"Then, let us pray," he exclaimed, with fervor, "that the hurricane has sunk the SERAPIS, and all on board."

Two hours later, the SERAPIS, showing she had met the hurricane and had come out second best, steamed into the harbor.

Her owner was young Herbert Livingstone, of Washington. He once had been in the diplomatic service, and, as minister to The Hague, wished to return to it. In order to bring this about he had subscribed liberally to the party campaign fund.

With him, among other distinguished persons, was the all-powerful Hanley. The kidnapping of Hanley for the cruise, in itself, demonstrated the ability of Livingstone as a diplomat. It was the opinion of many that it would surely lead to his appointment as a minister plenipotentiary. Livingstone was of the same opinion. He had not lived long in the nation's capital without observing the value of propinquity. How many men he knew were now paymasters, and secretaries of legation, solely because those high in the government met them daily at the Metropolitan Club, and preferred them in almost any other place. And if, after three weeks as his guest on board what the newspapers called his floating palace, the senator could refuse him even the prize, legation of Europe, there was no value in modest merit. As yet, Livingstone had not hinted at his ambition. There was no need. To a statesman of Hanley's astuteness, the largeness of Livingstone's contribution to the campaign fund was self-explanatory.

After her wrestling-match with the hurricane, all those on board the SERAPIS seemed to find in land, even in the swamp land of Porto Banos, a compelling attraction. Before the anchors hit the water, they were in the launch. On reaching shore, they made at once for the consulate. There were many cables they wished to start on their way by wireless; cables to friends, to newspapers, to the government.

Jose, the Colombian clerk, appalled by the unprecedented invasion of visitors, of visitors so distinguished, and Marshall, grateful for a chance to serve his fellow-countrymen, and especially his countrywomen, were ubiquitous, eager, indispensable. At Jose's desk the great senator, rolling his cigar between his teeth, was using, to Jose's ecstasy, Jose's own pen to write a reassuring message to the White House. At the consul's desk a beautiful creature, all in lace and pearls, was struggling to compress the very low opinion she held of a hurricane into ten words. On his knee, Henry Cairns, the banker, was inditing instructions to his Wall Street office, and upon himself Livingstone had taken the responsibility of replying to the inquiries heaped upon Marshall's desk, from many newspapers.

It was just before sunset, and Marshall produced his tea things, and the young person in pearls and lace, who was Miss Cairns, made tea for the women, and the men mixed gin and limes with tepid water. The consul apologized for proposing a toast in which they could not join. He begged to drink to those who had escaped the perils of the sea. Had they been his oldest and nearest friends, his little speech could not have been more heart-felt and sincere. To his distress, it moved one of the ladies to tears, and in embarrassment he turned to the men.

"I regret there is no ice," he said, "but you know the rule of the tropics; as soon as a ship enters port, the ice-machine bursts."

"I'll tell the steward to send you some, sir," said Livingstone, "and as long as we're here."

The senator showed his concern.

"As long as we're here?" he gasped.

"Not over two days," answered the owner nervously. "The chief says it will take all of that to get her in shape. As you ought to know, Senator, she was pretty badly mauled."

The senator gazed blankly out of the window. Beyond it lay the naked coral reefs, the empty sky, and the ragged palms of Porto Banos.

Livingstone felt that his legation was slipping from him.

"That wireless operator," he continued hastily, "tells me there is a most amusing place a few miles down the coast, Las Bocas, a sort of Coney Island, where the government people go for the summer. There's surf bathing and roulette and cafes chantants. He says there's some Spanish dancers----"

The guests of the SERAPIS exclaimed with interest; the senator smiled. To Marshall the general enthusiasm over the thought of a ride on a merry-go-round suggested that the friends of Mr. Livingstone had found their own society far from satisfying.

Greatly encouraged, Livingstone continued, with enthusiasm:

"And that wireless man said," he added, "that with the launch we can get there in half an hour. We might run down after dinner." He turned to Marshall.

"Will you join us, Mr. Consul?" he asked, "and dine with us, first?"

Marshall accepted with genuine pleasure. It had been many months since he had sat at table with his own people. But he shook his head doubtfully.

"I was wondering about Las Bocas," he explained, "if your going there might not get you in trouble at the next port. With a yacht, I think it is different, but Las Bocas is under quarantine."

There was a chorus of exclamations.

"It's not serious," Marshall explained. "There was bubonic plague there, or something like it. You would be in no danger from that. It is only that you might be held up by the regulations. Passenger steamers can't land any one who has been there at any other port of the West Indies. The English are especially strict. The Royal Mail won't even receive any one on board here without a certificate from the English consul saying he has not visited Las Bocas. For an American they would require the same guarantee from me. But I don't think the regulations extend to yachts. I will inquire. I don't wish to deprive you of any of the many pleasures of Porto Banos," he added, smiling, "but if you were refused a landing at your next port I would blame myself."

"It's all right," declared Livingstone decidedly. "It's just as you say; yachts and warships are exempt. Besides, I carry my own doctor, and if he won't give us a clean bill of health, I'll make him walk the plank. At eight, then, at dinner. I'll send the cutter for you. I can't give you a salute, Mr. Consul, but you shall have all the side boys I can muster."

Those from the yacht parted from their consul in the most friendly spirit.

"I think he's charming!" exclaimed Miss Cairns. "And did you notice his novels? They were in every language. It must be terribly lonely down here, for a man like that."

"He's the first of our consuls we've met on this trip," growled her father, "that we've caught sober."

"Sober!" exclaimed his wife indignantly.

"He's one of the Marshalls of Vermont. I asked him."

"I wonder," mused Hanley, "how much the place is worth? Hamilton, one of the new senators, has been deviling the life out of me to send his son somewhere. Says if he stays in Washington he'll disgrace the family. I should think this place would drive any man to drink himself to death in three months, and young Hamilton, from what I've seen of him, ought to be able to do it in a week. That would leave the place open for the next man."

"There's a postmaster in my State thinks he carried it." The senator smiled grimly. "He has consumption, and wants us to give him a consulship in the tropics. I'll tell him I've seen Porto Banos, and that it's just the place for him."

The senator's pleasantry was not well received. But Miss Cairns alone had the temerity to speak of what the others were thinking.

"What would become of Mr. Marshall?" she asked. The senator smiled tolerantly.

"I don't know that I was thinking of Mr. Marshall," he said. "I can't recall anything he has done for this administration. You see, Miss Cairns," he explained, in the tone of one addressing a small child, "Marshall has been abroad now for forty years, at the expense of the taxpayers. Some of us think men who have lived that long on their fellow-countrymen had better come home and get to work."

Livingstone nodded solemnly in assent. He did not wish a post abroad at the expense of the taxpayers. He was willing to pay for it. And then, with "ex-Minister" on his visiting cards, and a sense of duty well performed, for the rest of his life he could join the other expatriates in Paris.

Just before dinner, the cruiser RALEIGH having discovered the whereabouts of the SERAPIS by wireless, entered the harbor, and Admiral Hardy came to the yacht to call upon the senator, in whose behalf he had been scouring the Caribbean

Seas. Having paid his respects to that personage, the admiral fell boisterously upon Marshall.

The two old gentlemen were friends of many years. They had met, officially and unofficially, in many strange parts of the world. To each the chance reunion was a piece of tremendous good fortune. And throughout dinner the guests of Livingstone, already bored with each other, found in them and their talk of former days new and delightful entertainment. So much so that when, Marshall having assured them that the local quarantine regulations did not extend to a yacht, the men departed for Las Bocas, the women insisted that he and admiral remain behind.

It was for Marshall a wondrous evening. To foregather with his old friend whom he had known since Hardy was a mad midshipman, to sit at the feet of his own charming countrywomen, to listen to their soft, modulated laughter, to note how quickly they saw that to him the evening was a great event, and with what tact each contributed to make it the more memorable; all served to wipe out the months of bitter loneliness, the stigma of failure, the sense of undeserved neglect. In the moonlight, on the cool quarter-deck, they sat, in a half-circle, each of the two friends telling tales out of school, tales of which the other was the hero or the victim, "inside" stories of great occasions, ceremonies, bombardments, unrecorded "shirt-sleeve" diplomacy.

Hardy had helped to open the Suez Canal. Marshall had assisted the Queen of Madagascar to escape from the French invaders. On the Barbary Coast Hardy had chased pirates. In Edinburgh Marshall had played chess with Carlyle. He had seen Paris in mourning in the days of the siege, Paris in terror in the days of the Commune; he had known Garibaldi, Gambetta, the younger Dumas, the creator of Pickwick.

"Do you remember that time in Tangier," the admiral urged, "when I was a midshipman, and got into the bashaw's harem?"

"Do you remember how I got you out?" Marshall replied grimly.

"And," demanded Hardy, "do you remember when Adelina Patti paid a visit to the KEARSARGE at Marseilles in '65--George Dewey was our second officer--and you were bowing and backing away from her, and you backed into an open hatch, and she said 'my French isn't up to it' what was it she said?"

"I didn't hear it," said Marshall; "I was too far down the hatch."

"Do you mean the old KEARSARGE?" asked Mrs. Cairns. "Were you in the service then, Mr. Marshall?"

With loyal pride in his friend, the admiral answered for him:

"He was our consul-general at Marseilles!"

There was an uncomfortable moment. Even those denied imagination could not escape the contrast, could see in their mind's eye the great harbor of Marseilles, crowded with the shipping of the world, surrounding it the beautiful city, the rival of Paris to the north, and on the battleship the young consul-general making his bow to the young Empress of Song. And now, before their actual eyes, they saw the village of Porto Banos, a black streak in the night, a row of mud shacks, at the end of the wharf a single lantern yellow in the clear moonlight.

Later in the evening Miss Cairns led the admiral to one side.

"Admiral," she began eagerly, "tell me about your friend. Why is he here? Why don't they give him a place worthy of him? I've seen many of our representatives abroad, and I know we cannot afford to waste men like that." The girl exclaimed indignantly: "He's one of the most interesting men I've ever met! He's lived every-where, known every one. He's a distinguished man, a cultivated man; even I can see he knows his work, that he's a diplomat, born, trained, that he's----" The admiral interrupted with a growl.

"You don't have to tell ME about Henry," he protested. "I've known Henry twenty-five years. If Henry got his deserts," he exclaimed hotly, "he wouldn't be a consul on this coral reef; he'd be a minister in Europe. Look at me! We're the same age. We started together. When Lincoln sent him to Morocco as consul, he signed my commission as a midshipman. Now I'm an admiral. Henry has twice my brains and he's been a consul-general, and he's HERE, back at the foot of the ladder!"

"Why?" demanded the girl.

"Because the navy is a service and the consular service isn't a service. Men like Senator Hanley use it to pay their debts. While Henry's been serving his country abroad, he's lost his friends, lost his 'pull.' Those politicians up at Washington have no use for him. They don't consider that a consul like Henry can make a million dollars for his countrymen. He can keep them from shipping goods where there's no market, show them where there is a market." The admiral snorted contemptu-ously. "You don't have to tell ME the value of a good consul. But those politicians don't consider that. They only see that he has a job worth a few hundred dollars, and they want it, and if he hasn't other politicians to protect him, they'll take it." The girl raised her head.

"Why don't you speak to the senator?" she asked. "Tell him you've known him for years, that----"

"Glad to do it!" exclaimed the admiral heartily. "It won't be the first time. But Henry mustn't know. He's too confoundedly touchy. He hates the IDEA of influence, hates men like Hanley, who abuse it. If he thought anything was given to him except on his merits, he wouldn't take it."

"Then we won't tell him," said the girl. For a moment she hesitated.

"If I spoke to Mr. Hanley," she asked, "told him what I learned to-night of Mr. Marshall, would it have any effect?"

"Don't know how it will affect Hanley," said the sailor, "but if you asked me to make anybody a consul-general, I'd make him an ambassador."

Later in the evening Hanley and Livingstone were seated alone on deck. The visit to Las Bocas had not proved amusing, but, much to Livingstone's relief, his honored guest was now in good-humor. He took his cigar from his lips, only to sip at a long cool drink. He was in a mood flatteringly confidential and communicative.

"People have the strangest idea of what I can do for them," he laughed. It was his pose to pretend he was without authority. "They believe I've only to wave a wand, and get them anything they want. I thought I'd be safe from them on board a yacht."

Livingstone, in ignorance of what was coming, squirmed apprehensively.

"But it seems," the senator went on, "I'm at the mercy of a conspiracy. The women folk want me to do something for this fellow Marshall. If they had their way, they'd send him to the Court of St. James. And old Hardy, too, tackled me about him. So did Miss Cairns. And then Marshall himself got me behind the wheel-house, and I thought he was going to tell me how good he was, too! But he didn't."

As though the joke were on himself, the senator laughed appreciatively.

"Told me, instead, that Hardy ought to be a vice-admiral."

Livingstone, also, laughed, with the satisfied air of one who cannot be tricked.

"They fixed it up between them," he explained, "each was to put in a good word for the other." He nodded eagerly. "That's what I think."

There were moments during the cruise when Senator Hanley would have found relief in dropping his host overboard. With mock deference, the older man inclined his head.

"That's what you think, is it?" he asked. "Livingstone," he added, "you certainly are a great judge of men!"

The next morning, old man Marshall woke with a lightness at his heart that had been long absent. For a moment, conscious only that he was happy, he lay between sleep and waking, frowning up at his canopy of mosquito net, trying to realize what change had come to him. Then he remembered. His old friend had returned. New friends had come into his life and welcomed him kindly. He was no longer lonely. As eager as a boy, he ran to the window. He had not been dreaming. In the harbor lay the pretty yacht, the stately, white-hulled war-ship. The flag that drooped from the stern of each caused his throat to tighten, brought warm tears to his eyes, fresh resolve to his discouraged, troubled spirit. When he knelt beside his bed, his heart poured out his thanks in gratitude and gladness.

While he was dressing, a blue-jacket brought a note from the admiral. It invited him to tea on board the war-ship, with the guests of the SERAPIS. His old friend added that he was coming to lunch with his consul, and wanted time reserved for a long talk. The consul agreed gladly. He was in holiday humor. The day promised to repeat the good moments of the night previous.

At nine o'clock, through the open door of the consulate, Marshall saw Aiken, the wireless operator, signaling from the wharf excitedly to the yacht, and a boat leave the ship and return. Almost immediately the launch, carrying several passengers, again made the trip shoreward.

Half an hour later, Senator Hanley, Miss Cairns, and Livingstone came up the waterfront, and entering the consulate, seated themselves around Marshall's desk. Livingstone was sunk in melancholy. The senator, on the contrary, was smiling broadly. His manner was one of distinct relief. He greeted the consul with hearty good-humor.

"I'm ordered home!" he announced gleefully. Then, remembering the presence of Livingstone, he hastened to add: "I needn't say how sorry I am to give up my yachting trip, but orders are orders. The President," he explained to Marshall, "cables me this morning to come back and take my coat off." The prospect, as a change from playing bridge on a pleasure boat, seemed far from depressing him.

"Those filibusters in the Senate," he continued genially, "are making trouble again. They think they've got me out of the way for another month, but they'll find they're wrong. When that bill comes up, they'll find me at the old stand and ready for business!" Marshall did not attempt to conceal his personal disappointment.

"I am so sorry you are leaving," he said; "selfishly sorry, I mean. I'd hoped you all would be here for several days." He looked inquiringly toward Livingstone.

"I understood the SERAPIS was disabled," he explained.

"She is," answered Hanley. "So's the RALEIGH. At a pinch, the admiral might have stretched the regulations and carried me to Jamaica, but the RALEIGH's engines are knocked about too. I've GOT to reach Kingston Thursday. The German boat leaves there Thursday for New York. At first it looked as though I couldn't do it, but we find that the Royal Mail is due to-day, and she can get to Kingston Wednesday night. It's a great piece of luck. I wouldn't bother you with my troubles," the senator explained pleasantly, "but the agent of the Royal Mail here won't sell me a ticket until you've put your seal to this." He extended a piece of printed paper.

As Hanley had been talking, the face of the consul had grown grave. He accepted the paper, but did not look at it. Instead, he regarded the senator with troubled eyes. When he spoke, his tone was one of genuine concern.

"It is most unfortunate," he said. "But I am afraid the ROYAL MAIL will not take you on board. Because of Las Bocas," he explained. "If we had only known!" he added remorsefully. "It is MOST unfortunate."

"Because of Las Bocas?" echoed Hanley.

"You don't mean they'll refuse to take me to Jamaica because I spent half an hour at the end of a wharf listening to a squeaky gramophone?"

"The trouble," explained Marshall, "is this: if they carried you, all the other passengers would be held in quarantine for ten days, and there are fines to pay, and there would be difficulties over the mails. But," he added hopefully, "maybe the regulations have been altered. I will see her captain, and tell him----"

"See her captain!" objected Hanley. "Why see the captain? He doesn't know I've been to that place. Why tell him? All I need is a clean bill of health from you. That's all HE wants. You have only to sign that paper." Marshall regarded the senator with surprise.

"But I can't," he said.

"You can't? Why not?"

"Because it certifies to the fact that you have not visited Las Bocas. Unfortunately, you have visited Las Bocas."

The senator had been walking up and down the room. Now he seated himself, and stared at Marshall curiously.

"It's like this, Mr. Marshall," he began quietly. "The President desires my presence in Washington, thinks I can be of some use to him there in helping carry out certain party measures--measures to which he pledged himself before his election. Down here, a British steamship line has laid down local rules which, in my case anyway, are ridiculous. The question is, are you going to be bound by the red tape of a ha'penny British colony, or by your oath to the President of the United States?"

The sophistry amused Marshall. He smiled good-naturedly and shook his head.

"I'm afraid, Senator," he said, "that way of putting it is hardly fair. Unfortunately, the question is one of fact. I will explain to the captain----"

"You will explain nothing to the captain!" interrupted Hanley. "This is a matter which concerns no one but our two selves. I am not asking favors of steamboat captains. I am asking an American consul to assist an American citizen in trouble, and," he added, with heavy sarcasm, "incidentally, to carry out the wishes of his President."

Marshall regarded the senator with an expression of both surprise and disbelief.

"Are you asking me to put my name to what is not so?" he said. "Are you serious?"

"That paper, Mr. Marshall," returned Hanley steadily, "is a mere form, a piece of red tape. There's no more danger of my carrying the plague to Jamaica than of my carrying a dynamite bomb. You KNOW that."

"I DO know that," assented Marshall heartily. "I appreciate your position, and I regret it exceedingly. You are the innocent victim of a regulation which is a wise regulation, but which is most unfair to you. My own position," he added, "is not important, but you can believe me, it is not easy. It is certainly no pleasure for me to be unable to help you."

Hanley was leaning forward, his hands on his knees, his eyes watching Marshall closely. "Then you refuse?" he said. "Why?"

Marshall regarded the senator steadily. His manner was untroubled. The look he turned upon Hanley was one of grave disapproval.

"You know why," he answered quietly. "It is impossible."

In sudden anger Hanley rose. Marshall, who had been seated behind his desk, also rose. For a moment, in silence, the two men confronted each other. Then Hanley spoke; his tone was harsh and threatening.

"Then I am to understand," he exclaimed, "that you refuse to carry out the wishes of a United States Senator and of the President of the United States?"

In front of Marshall, on his desk, was the little iron stamp of the consulate. Protectingly, almost caressingly, he laid his hand upon it.

"I refuse," he corrected, "to place the seal of this consulate on a lie."

There was a moment's pause. Miss Cairns, unwilling to remain, and unable to withdraw, clasped her hands unhappily and stared at the floor. Livingstone exclaimed in indignant protest. Hanley moved a step nearer and, to emphasize what he said, tapped his knuckles on the desk. With the air of one confident of his advantage, he spoke slowly and softly.

"Do you appreciate," he asked, "that, while you may be of some importance down here in this fever swamp, in Washington I am supposed to carry some weight? Do you appreciate that I am a senator from a State that numbers four millions of people, and that you are preventing me from serving those people?" Marshall inclined his head gravely and politely.

"And I want you to appreciate," he said, "that while I have no weight at Washington, in this fever swamp I have the honor to represent eighty millions of people, and as long as that consular sign is over my door I don't intend to prostitute it for YOU, or the President of the United States, or any one of those eighty millions."

Of the two men, the first to lower his eyes was Hanley. He laughed shortly, and walked to the door. There he turned, and indifferently, as though the incident no longer interested him, drew out his watch.

"Mr. Marshall," he said, "if the cable is working, I'll take your tin sign away from you by sunset."

For one of Marshall's traditions, to such a speech there was no answer save silence. He bowed, and, apparently serene and undismayed, resumed his seat. From the contest, judging from the manner of each, it was Marshall, not Hanley, who had emerged victorious.

But Miss Cairns was not deceived. Under the unexpected blow, Marshall had turned older. His clear blue eyes had grown less alert, his broad shoulders seemed to stoop. In sympathy, her own eyes filled with sudden tears.

"What will you do?" she whispered.

"I don't know what I shall do," said Marshall simply. "I should have liked to have resigned. It's a prettier finish. After forty years--to be dismissed by cable is--it's a poor way of ending it."

Miss Cairns rose and walked to the door. There she turned and looked back.

"I am sorry," she said. And both understood that in saying no more than that she had best shown her sympathy.

An hour later the sympathy of Admiral Hardy was expressed more directly.

"If he comes on board my ship," roared that gentleman, "I'll push him down an ammunition hoist and break his damned neck!"

Marshall laughed delightedly. The loyalty of his old friend was never so welcome.

"You'll treat him with every courtesy," he said. "The only satisfaction he gets out of this is to see that he has hurt me. We will not give him that satisfaction."

But Marshall found that to conceal his wound was more difficult than he had anticipated. When, at tea time, on the deck of the war-ship, he again met Senator Hanley and the guests of the SERAPIS, he could not forget that his career had come to an end. There was much to remind him that this was so. He was made aware of it by the sad, sympathetic glances of the women; by their tactful courtesies; by the fact that Livingstone, anxious to propitiate Hanley, treated him rudely; by the sight of the young officers, each just starting upon a career of honor, and possible glory, as his career ended in humiliation; and by the big war-ship herself, that recalled certain crises when he had only to press a button and war-ships had come at his bidding.

At five o'clock there was an awkward moment. The Royal Mail boat, having taken on her cargo, passed out of the harbor on her way to Jamaica, and dipped her colors. Senator Hanley, abandoned to his fate, observed her departure in silence.

Livingstone, hovering at his side, asked sympathetically: "Have they answered your cable, sir?"

"They have," said Hanley gruffly.

"Was it--was it satisfactory?" pursued the diplomat.

"It WAS," said the senator, with emphasis.

Far from discouraged, Livingstone continued his inquiries.

"And when," he asked eagerly, "are you going to tell him?"

"Now!" said the senator.

The guests were leaving the ship. When all were seated in the admiral's steam launch, the admiral descended the accommodation ladder and himself picked up the tiller ropes.

"Mr. Marshall," he called, "when I bring the launch broadside to the ship and stop her, you will stand ready to receive the consul's salute."

Involuntarily, Marshall uttered an exclamation of protest. He had forgotten that on leaving the war-ship, as consul, he was entitled to seven guns. Had he re-membered, he would have insisted that the ceremony be omitted. He knew that the admiral wished to show his loyalty, knew that his old friend was now paying him this honor only as a rebuke to Hanley. But the ceremony was no longer an honor. Hanley had made of it a mockery. It served only to emphasize what had been taken from him. But, without a scene, it now was too late to avoid it. The first of the seven guns had roared from the bow, and, as often he had stood before, as never he would so stand again, Marshall took his place at the gangway of the launch. His eyes were fixed on the flag, his gray head was uncovered, his hat was pressed above his heart.

For the first time since Hanley had left the consulate, he fell into sudden terror lest he might give way to his emotions. Indignant at the thought, he held himself erect. His face was set like a mask, his eyes were untroubled. He was determined they should not see that he was suffering.

Another gun spat out a burst of white smoke, a stab of flame. There was an echoing roar. Another and another followed. Marshall counted seven, and then, with a bow to the admiral, backed from the gangway.

And then another gun shattered the hot, heavy silence. Marshall, confused, embarrassed, assuming he had counted wrong, hastily returned to his place. But again before he could leave it, in savage haste a ninth gun roared out its greeting. He could not still be mistaken. He turned appealingly to his friend. The eyes of the admiral were fixed upon the war-ship. Again a gun shattered the silence. Was it a jest? Were they laughing at him? Marshall flushed miserably. He gave a swift glance toward the others. They were smiling. Then it was a jest. Behind his back, something of which they all were cognizant was going forward. The face of Livingstone alone betrayed a like bewilderment to his own. But the others, who knew, were mocking him.

For the thirteenth time a gun shook the brooding swamp land of Porto Banos. And then, and not until then, did the flag crawl slowly from the mast-head. Mary Cairns broke the tenseness by bursting into tears. But Marshall saw that every one else, save she and Livingstone, were still smiling. Even the bluejackets in charge of the launch were grinning at him. He was beset by smiling faces. And then from the war-ship, unchecked, came, against all regulations, three long, splendid cheers.

Marshall felt his lips quivering, the warm tears forcing their way to his eyes. He turned beseechingly to his friend. His voice trembled.

"Charles," he begged, "are they laughing at me?"

Eagerly, before the other would answer, Senator Hanley tossed his cigar into the water and, scrambling forward, seized Marshall by the hand.

"Mr. Marshall," he cried, "our President has great faith in Abraham Lincoln's judgment of men. And this salute means that this morning he appointed you our new minister to The Hague. I'm one of those politicians who keeps his word. I TOLD YOU I'd take your tin sign away from you by sunset. I've done it!"

www.bookjungle.com *email: sales@bookjungle.com fax: 630-214-0564 mail: Book Jungle PO Box 2226 Champaign, IL 61825*

The Codes Of Hammurabi And Moses
W. W. Davies

QTY

The discovery of the Hammurabi Code is one of the greatest achievements of archaeology, and is of paramount interest, not only to the student of the Bible, but also to all those interested in ancient history...

Religion   **ISBN: *1-59462-338-4***   **Pages:132**
MSRP $12.95

The Theory of Moral Sentiments
Adam Smith

QTY

This work from 1749. contains original theories of conscience amd moral judgment and it is the foundation for systemof morals.

Philosophy **ISBN: *1-59462-777-0***   **Pages:536**
MSRP $19.95

Jessica's First Prayer
Hesba Stretton

QTY

In a screened and secluded corner of one of the many railway-bridges which span the streets of London there could be seen a few years ago, from five o'clock every morning until half past eight, a tidily set-out coffee-stall, consisting of a trestle and board, upon which stood two large tin cans, with a small fire of charcoal burning under each so as to keep the coffee boiling during the early hours of the morning when the work-people were thronging into the city on their way to their daily toil...

Childrens   **ISBN: *1-59462-373-2***   **Pages:84**
MSRP $9.95

My Life and Work
Henry Ford

QTY

Henry Ford revolutionized the world with his implementation of mass production for the Model T automobile. Gain valuable business insight into his life and work with his own auto-biography... "We have only started on our development of our country we have not as yet, with all our talk of wonderful progress, done more than scratch the surface. The progress has been wonderful enough but..."

Biographies/ **ISBN: *1-59462-198-5***   **Pages:300**
MSRP $21.95

The Art of Cross-Examination
Francis Wellman

QTY

I presume it is the experience of every author, after his first book is published upon an important subject, to be almost overwhelmed with a wealth of ideas and illustrations which could readily have been included in his book, and which to his own mind, at least, seem to make a second edition inevitable. Such certainly was the case with me; and when the first edition had reached its sixth impression in five months, I rejoiced to learn that it seemed to my publishers that the book had met with a sufficiently favorable reception to justify a second and considerably enlarged edition. ...

Pages:412

Reference   ISBN: *1-59462-647-2*   *MSRP $19.95*

On the Duty of Civil Disobedience
Henry David Thoreau

QTY

Thoreau wrote his famous essay, On the Duty of Civil Disobedience, as a protest against an unjust but popular war and the immoral but popular institution of slave-owning. He did more than write—he declined to pay his taxes, and was hauled off to gaol in consequence. Who can say how much this refusal of his hastened the end of the war and of slavery ?

Law   ISBN: *1-59462-747-9*   **Pages:48**

MSRP $7.45

Dream Psychology
Psychoanalysis for Beginners

Sigmund Freud

Dream Psychology Psychoanalysis for Beginners
Sigmund Freud

QTY

Sigmund Freud, born Sigismund Schlomo Freud (May 6, 1856 - September 23, 1939), was a Jewish-Austrian neurologist and psychiatrist who co-founded the psychoanalytic school of psychology. Freud is best known for his theories of the unconscious mind, especially involving the mechanism of repression; his redefinition of sexual desire as mobile and directed towards a wide variety of objects; and his therapeutic techniques, especially his understanding of transference in the therapeutic relationship and the presumed value of dreams as sources of insight into unconscious desires.

Pages:196

Psychology   ISBN: *1-59462-905-6*   *MSRP $15.45*

The Miracle of Right Thought
Orison Swett Marden

QTY

Believe with all of your heart that you will do what you were made to do. When the mind has once formed the habit of holding cheerful, happy, prosperous pictures, it will not be easy to form the opposite habit. It does not matter how improbable or how far away this realization may see, or how dark the prospects may be, if we visualize them as best we can, as vividly as possible, hold tenaciously to them and vigorously struggle to attain them, they will gradually become actualized, realized in the life. But a desire, a longing without endeavor, a yearning abandoned or held indifferently will vanish without realization.

Pages:360

Self Help   ISBN: *1-59462-644-8*   *MSRP $25.45*

QTY

The Rosicrucian Cosmo-Conception Mystic Christianity *by Max Heindel*   ISBN: *1-59462-188-8*   **$38.95**
The Rosicrucian Cosmo-conception is not dogmatic, neither does it appeal to any other authority than the reason of the student. It is: not controversial, but is: sent forth in the, hope that it may help to clear...   *New Age/Religion Pages 646*

Abandonment To Divine Providence *by Jean-Pierre de Caussade*   ISBN: *1-59462-228-0*   **$25.95**
"The Rev. Jean Pierre de Caussade was one of the most remarkable spiritual writers of the Society of Jesus in France in the 18th Century. His death took place at Toulouse in 1751. His works have gone through many editions and have been republished...   *Inspirational/Religion Pages 400*

Mental Chemistry *by Charles Haanel*   ISBN: *1-59462-192-6*   **$23.95**
Mental Chemistry allows the change of material conditions by combining and appropriately utilizing the power of the mind. Much like applied chemistry creates something new and unique out of careful combinations of chemicals the mastery of mental chemistry...   *New Age Pages 354*

The Letters of Robert Browning and Elizabeth Barret Barrett 1845-1846 vol II   ISBN: *1-59462-193-4*   **$35.95**
by Robert Browning and Elizabeth Barrett   *Biographies Pages 596*

Gleanings In Genesis (volume I) *by Arthur W. Pink*   ISBN: *1-59462-130-6*   **$27.45**
Appropriately has Genesis been termed "the seed plot of the Bible" for in it we have, in germ form, almost all of the great doctrines which are afterwards fully developed in the books of Scripture which follow...   *Religion/Inspirational Pages 420*

The Master Key *by L. W. de Laurence*   ISBN: *1-59462-001-6*   **$30.95**
In no branch of human knowledge has there been a more lively increase of the spirit of research during the past few years than in the study of Psychology, Concentration and Mental Discipline. The requests for authentic lessons in Thought Control, Mental Discipline and...   *New Age/Business Pages 422*

The Lesser Key Of Solomon Goetia *by L. W. de Laurence*   ISBN: *1-59462-092-X*   **$9.95**
This translation of the first book of the "Lernegton" which is now for the first time made accessible to students of Talismanic Magic was done, after careful collation and edition, from numerous Ancient Manuscripts in Hebrew, Latin, and French...   *New Age/Occult Pages 92*

Rubaiyat Of Omar Khayyam *by Edward Fitzgerald*   ISBN:*1-59462-332-5*   **$13.95**
Edward Fitzgerald, whom the world has already learned, in spite of his own efforts to remain within the shadow of anonymity, to look upon as one of the rarest poets of the century, was born at Bredfield, in Suffolk, on the 31st of March, 1809. He was the third son of John Purcell...   *Music Pages 172*

Ancient Law *by Henry Maine*   ISBN: *1-59462-128-4*   **$29.95**
The chief object of the following pages is to indicate some of the earliest ideas of mankind, as they are reflected in Ancient Law, and to point out the relation of those ideas to modern thought.   *Religion/History Pages 452*

Far-Away Stories *by William J. Locke*   ISBN: *1-59462-129-2*   **$19.45**
"Good wine needs no bush, but a collection of mixed vintages does. And this book is just such a collection. Some of the stories I do not want to remain buried for ever in the museum files of dead magazine-numbers an author's not unpardonable vanity..."   *Fiction Pages 272*

Life of David Crockett *by David Crockett*   ISBN: *1-59462-250-7*   **$27.45**
"Colonel David Crockett was one of the most remarkable men of the times in which he lived. Born in humble life, but gifted with a strong will, an indomitable courage, and unremitting perseverance...   *Biographies/New Age Pages 424*

Lip-Reading *by Edward Nitchie*   ISBN: *1-59462-206-X*   **$25.95**
Edward B. Nitchie, founder of the New York School for the Hard of Hearing, now the Nitchie School of Lip-Reading, Inc, wrote "LIP-READING Principles and Practice". The development and perfecting of this meritorious work on lip-reading was an undertaking...   *How-to Pages 400*

A Handbook of Suggestive Therapeutics, Applied Hypnotism, Psychic Science   ISBN: *1-59462-214-0*   **$24.95**
by Henry Munro   *Health/New Age/Health/Self-help Pages 376*

A Doll's House: and Two Other Plays *by Henrik Ibsen*   ISBN: *1-59462-112-8*   **$19.95**
Henrik Ibsen created this classic when in revolutionary 1848 Rome. Introducing some striking concepts in playwriting for the realist genre, this play has been studied the world over.   *Fiction/Classics/Plays 308*

The Light of Asia *by sir Edwin Arnold*   ISBN: *1-59462-204-3*   **$13.95**
In this poetic masterpiece, Edwin Arnold describes the life and teachings of Buddha. The man who was to become known as Buddha to the world was born as Prince Gautama of India but he rejected the worldly riches and abandoned the reigns of power when...   *Religion/History/Biographies Pages 170*

The Complete Works of Guy de Maupassant *by Guy de Maupassant*   ISBN: *1-59462-157-8*   **$16.95**
"For days and days, nights and nights, I had dreamed of that first kiss which was to consecrate our engagement, and I knew not on what spot I should put my lips..."   *Fiction/Classics Pages 240*

The Art of Cross-Examination *by Francis L. Wellman*   ISBN: *1-59462-309-0*   **$26.95**
Written by a renowned trial lawyer, Wellman imparts his experience and uses case studies to explain how to use psychology to extract desired information through questioning.   *How-to/Science/Reference Pages 408*

Answered or Unanswered? *by Louisa Vaughan*   ISBN: *1-59462-248-5*   **$10.95**
Miracles of Faith in China   *Religion Pages 112*

The Edinburgh Lectures on Mental Science (1909) *by Thomas*   ISBN: *1-59462-008-3*   **$11.95**
This book contains the substance of a course of lectures recently given by the writer in the Queen Street Hall, Edinburgh. Its purpose is to indicate the Natural Principles governing the relation between Mental Action and Material Conditions...   *New Age/Psychology Pages 148*

Ayesha *by H. Rider Haggard*   ISBN: *1-59462-301-5*   **$24.95**
Verily and indeed it is the unexpected that happens! Probably if there was one person upon the earth from whom the Editor of this, and of a certain previous history, did not expect to hear again...   *Classics Pages 380*

Ayala's Angel *by Anthony Trollope*   ISBN: *1-59462-352-X*   **$29.95**
The two girls were both pretty, but Lucy who was twenty-one who supposed to be simple and comparatively unattractive, whereas Ayala was credited, as her Bombwhat romantic name might show, with poetic charm and a taste for romance. Ayala when her father died was nineteen...   *Fiction Pages 484*

The American Commonwealth *by James Bryce*   ISBN: *1-59462-286-8*   **$34.45**
An interpretation of American democratic political theory. It examines political mechanics and society from the perspective of Scotsman James Bryce   *Politics Pages 572*

Stories of the Pilgrims *by Margaret P. Pumphrey*   ISBN: *1-59462-116-0*   **$17.95**
This book explores pilgrims religious oppression in England as well as their escape to Holland and eventual crossing to America on the Mayflower, and their early days in New England...   *History Pages 268*

QTY

The Fasting Cure *by Sinclair Upton*   ISBN: *1-59462-222-1* **$13.95**

In the Cosmopolitan Magazine for May, 1910, and in the Contemporary Review (London) for April, 1910, I published an article dealing with my experiences in fasting. I have written a great many magazine articles, but never one which attracted so much attention... New Age/Self Help/Health Pages 164

Hebrew Astrology *by Sepharial*   ISBN: *1-59462-308-2* **$13.45**

In these days of advanced thinking it is a matter of common observation that we have left many of the old landmarks behind and that we are now pressing forward to greater heights and to a wider horizon than that which represented the mind-content of our progenitors... Astrology Pages 144

Thought Vibration or The Law of Attraction in the Thought World   ISBN: *1-59462-127-6* **$12.95**

by William Walker Atkinson   *Psychology/Religion Pages 144*

Optimism *by Helen Keller*   ISBN: *1-59462-108-X* **$15.95**

Helen Keller was blind, deaf, and mute since 19 months old, yet famously learned how to overcome these handicaps, communicate with the world, and spread her lectures promoting optimism. An inspiring read for everyone... Biographies/Inspirational Pages 84

Sara Crewe *by Frances Burnett*   ISBN: *1-59462-360-0* **$9.45**

In the first place, Miss Minchin lived in London. Her home was a large, dull, tall one, in a large, dull square, where all the houses were alike, and all the sparrows were alike, and where all the door-knockers made the same heavy sound... Childrens/Classic Pages 88

The Autobiography of Benjamin Franklin *by Benjamin Franklin*   ISBN: *1-59462-135-7* **$24.95**

The Autobiography of Benjamin Franklin has probably been more extensively read than any other American historical work, and no other book of its kind has had such ups and downs of fortune. Franklin lived for many years in England, where he was agent... Biographies/History Pages 332

Name	
Email	
Telephone	
Address	
City, State ZIP	

☐ **Credit Card**   ☐ **Check / Money Order**

Credit Card Number	
Expiration Date	
Signature	

Please Mail to: Book Jungle
PO Box 2226
Champaign, IL 61825
or Fax to: 630-214-0564

ORDERING INFORMATION

web: *www.bookjungle.com*
email: *sales@bookjungle.com*
fax: *630-214-0564*
mail: *Book Jungle PO Box 2226 Champaign, IL 61825*
or PayPal *to sales@bookjungle.com*

Please contact us for bulk discounts

DIRECT-ORDER TERMS

**20% Discount if You Order
Two or More Books**
Free Domestic Shipping!
Accepted: Master Card, Visa,
Discover, American Express

www.ingramcontent.com/pod-product-compliance
Lightning Source LLC
Chambersburg PA
CBHW081203170626

46813CB00009B/3308